REALM OF
MYSTICS

LEVEL UP

REALM OF MYSTICS

RAELYN DRAKE

darbycreek

MINNEAPOLIS

Darby Creek
A division of Lerner Publishing Group, Inc.
241 First Avenue North
Minneapolis, MN 55401 USA

For reading levels and more information, look up this title at
www.lernerbooks.com.

Images in this book used with the permission of: © Melkor3D/Shutterstock.com (dragon), © iStockphoto.com/trendobjects (snow background), © iStockphoto.com/ Thoth_Andan (grunge background).

Main body text set in Janson Text LT Std 12/17.5.
Typeface provided by Adobe Systems.

Library of Congress Cataloging-in-Publication Data

The Cataloging-in-Publication Data for Realm of Mystics is on file at the Library of Congress.
ISBN 978-1-5124-3989-2 (lib. bdg.)
ISBN 978-1-5124-5359-1 (pbk.)
ISBN 978-1-5124-4878-8 (EB pdf)

Manufactured in the United States of America
1-42238-25787-3/15/2017

To my husband

It is the year 2089. Virtual reality games are part of everyday life, and one company—L33T CORP—is behind the most popular games. Though most people are familiar with L33T CORP, few know much about what happens behind the scenes of the megacorporation.

L33T CORP has developed a new virtual reality game: *Level Up*. It contains more than one thousand unique virtual realities for gamers to play. But the company needs testers to smooth out glitches. Teenagers from around the country are chosen for this task and, suddenly, they find themselves in the middle of a video game. The company gives them a warning—win the game, or be trapped within it. Forever.

CHAPTER 1

"Welcome to *Level Up*."

Eyes still closed, the player tried to slap the snooze button on her alarm, but her hand met only rough wood.

"Congratulations! You have been randomly selected to beta test the *Realm of Mystics* scenario of our new game, *Level Up*. L33T C0RP thanks you for your participation."

The player's eyes snapped open.

A middle-aged man in a white suit and sunglasses stared down at her. He smiled, and his teeth glinted a brighter white than his suit. The player had a feeling that the smile didn't reach the eyes behind those dark lenses.

She lay on the floor of some sort of wooden shack. She tried to remember how she had gotten there, but everything was blank. "What's going on?" She sat up, pressing a hand to her aching forehead.

"Do you need me to repeat the welcome message again? I thought it explained the situation rather nicely."

"No, I just—"

The man flickered, pixelated, then snapped back.

She blinked a few times. "Did you just—are you a hologram or something?"

"I'm the Game Runner," he said, as though he was stating something obvious. The player would have found the man's smug tone annoying under normal circumstances. "This is my avatar in *Level Up*. As you can see, there are still a few glitches to work out." He smacked the side of his head as if he was trying to get water out of his ear. "That's why we need beta testers before we release *Level Up* to the general public."

The player suddenly realized why this all sounded so familiar. She remembered seeing a headline in her news feed that L33T C0RP would soon be releasing a fully immersive virtual reality gaming experience. She hadn't bothered to read the article. She had never been great at video games.

"What if I don't want to be a beta tester?"

"You already signed a contract," the Game Runner said.

She frowned. "I don't remember doing that."

The Game Runner smiled again—it seemed to be his default expression—and shrugged. "Memories are often misplaced during the login process—"

A door at the back of the shack burst open. A girl the same age as the player appeared, her long black hair arranged in dozens of tiny braids.

"Hey, let's get going already." She pulled her braids back into a ponytail. The player noticed text floating above the girl's head: Rox_Ur_Sox. *That must be her name in the game*, she thought. The text disappeared after she had a moment to read it.

Rox_Ur_Sox wore cherry-red armor that gleamed in the last rays of sun shining through the shack's windows. The player looked down at her own clothes. She was dressed in midnight blue robes, belted at the waist and sprinkled with silver sequins like stars. "What the—?"

Two boys followed Rox_Ur_Sox into the room. The boy with tousled black hair wore a knee-length brown leather coat. Floating above his head was the name E1_Kapitan. The skinny redheaded boy in a black hooded cloak—D4rkHunter—knelt to finish lacing up his boots.

"What kind of video game *is* this?" the player asked.

Rox_Ur_Sox raised an eyebrow. "Oh no, don't tell me you're a n00b . . ."

"A what?"

D4rkHunter whispered behind his hand like he was sharing a secret with her. "Gamer slang for 'newbie.' She means you've never really played video games before."

She shrugged. "Do phone games count?"

Rox_Ur_Sox rolled her eyes and sighed. "Can we just get started?"

"This player just needs to select her gamertag," the Game Runner said, gesturing to the player. Everyone turned to look at her.

"My what?"

"This is the name you will go by in the game. Everyone else has already chosen theirs."

"Umm—"

"Time's up," the Game Runner said. "A gamertag has been generated for you. Welcome to *Realm of Mystics*, Em3ra1d_with_3nvy."

Em3ra1d_with_3nvy noticed E1_Kapitan staring at a spot above her head. She looked up and saw her new name floating above her. It too disappeared after a moment.

"Em3ra1d_with_3nvy," he repeated. "That's not a bad gamertag for a n00b."

"*Envy* is right, when she sees how real gamers play." Rox_Ur_Sox smirked.

"Can we call her Em3ra1d for short?" E1_Kapitan asked the others. "That name is kind of a mouthful."

"Do you all know each other?" Em3ra1d

asked, still trying to wrap her head around the situation.

D4rkHunter shook his head. "Not in real life. Kap and I hang out on the L33T C0RP gaming forums, but I've never met him offline. You and Roxy are new."

"I'm not *new*," scoffed Rox_Ur_Sox. "I just don't waste my time by socializing with other gamers." She turned to the Game Runner expectantly. "I'll feel better once I get to fight something."

The Game Runner smiled. "Your quest," he explained, "is to complete four levels— Water Level, Earth Level, Fire Level, and Air Level. These challenges have been designed to test your deepest fears and take advantage of your unique strengths. If you complete those four levels, you will then face the Boss Battle level, which you will beat by releasing the princess and defeating the dragon."

"Sounds simple enough," D4rkHunter said.

Em3ra1d snorted. "Sure. *Simple.*"

"You have all been assigned weapons based on your type of character in *Realm of Mystics*," the Game Runner said. "Rox_Ur_Sox, you are a Warrior, so you get a sword and shield."

"Sweet!" Rox_Ur_Sox said. The sword and shield appeared in her hand out of thin air. She slashed the blade experimentally, with the round wooden shield strapped to her opposite arm for defense.

"D4rkHunter, as a Ranger, you will get a bow and arrows."

D4rkHunter slung his newly acquired quiver full of arrows over his back and tested how far he could bend the wooden bow. He nodded approvingly.

"E1_Kapitan, you are a Druid—"

"What's a Druid?" Em3ra1d asked.

"Druids have the power to control nature," the Game Runner explained. "E1_Kapitan will use a magic staff."

E1_Kapitan took the wooden staff, which was nearly as tall as he was, and thumped the floorboards with the butt end. A vine with spiky black flowers sprouted from the top, curling and coiling down the length of the staff.

"Cool," El_Kapitan said, nudging D4rkHunter and smiling.

"Em3ra1d_with_3nvy, you are a Mage—a magic user—and you get this spell book." The Game Runner handed her a leather-bound book.

Rox_Ur_Sox groaned. "The n00b is the Mage? We're so screwed without a good Mage."

Em3ra1d flipped through the book. The spells all had names like *Fireball* and *Teleport*.

"I don't know if I feel very safe with only an old book to protect me. Didn't you say we were going to have to fight a dragon?"

The Game Runner seemed to ignore her. He handed them all leather wristbands. On each, a red crystal and a blue crystal glowed brightly. "Every time you get hurt, you lose Health. Your red Health crystal recharges slowly, but if you lose all of your Health before it can recharge, you die."

"What?" Em3ra1d exclaimed, her head jerking up from the spell book.

"We don't *actually* die, dummy," Rox_Ur_Sox said. "It's just video game death. You come back after you respawn."

"You each get three lives," the Game Runner continued. "When you die the third time, you lose; three strikes, you're out—you get the picture. The four of you together form a group called a 'party.' If all of you die at once, then everyone loses instantly. One or more of you can finish the game, but it will be much easier to win with all four party members."

Em3ra1d raised her hand. "So what's the blue crystal for?"

"Whenever you use a spell or a weapon, you use a bit of Power. Like your Health crystal, your blue Power crystal recharges slowly, so make sure you ration it out during battles."

The players nodded thoughtfully and attached their wristbands.

The Game Runner turned to Em3ra1d. "Why don't you try out a spell now? Aim your hand at where you want the spell to go and shout the name of the spell." He gestured to the blank stretch of wall next to him.

Em3ra1d looked at the spell book. The page was open to a spell called *Light*. She held out her hand toward the wall as if she was about to shoot lasers from her palm. *I probably look ridiculous*, she thought.

"*Light?*" she said. It was more of a question than a shout. She felt a blush creep into her cheeks.

A tiny sphere of golden light appeared suspended in the air between her and the wall. Then the light sputtered out with the squeaky whistling noise of a balloon deflating.

Rox_Ur_Sox groaned.

Em3rald felt that the Game Runner hesitated a moment too long before he exclaimed, "Good!" and flashed his insincere smile.

Em3rald looked at her wristband. The blue Power crystal had dimmed slightly.

"I'm afraid the rest of the tutorial isn't available in the beta version," the Game Runner said.

"But wait," Em3rald said, "I still don't get—"

The Game Runner ushered them out the door of the shack. "You'll just have to pick up the rest as you go."

LEVEL 1

WATER

CHAPTER 2

The players found themselves on a wooden pier that stretched away to either side of them, forming a half circle open to the ocean. Ten other shacks that looked identical to the one they had just left lined the pier. Here and there, wooden ladders slick with algae and sea spray descended from the pier into the murky water five feet below.

In front of them, the sun had just dipped below the ocean's horizon, streaking the sky with peach and lavender. Behind them, the first evening stars flecked the horizon. Beyond the pier, a forest rose toward a distant mountain peak ringed with smoke.

It all looked so real. A fresh sea breeze stirred her hair, carrying with it the tangy scent of salt and seaweed. It even *smelled* real. Em3ra1d could hardly believe this was *virtual* reality.

"Now don't forget," the Game Runner said from behind them, "the most important thing is having fun! Well, actually the most important thing is winning, because otherwise you can't leave the game. So have fun. But also win. Good luck!"

"Wait, *what*?" Em3ra1d turned around, but the Game Runner had vanished. "What did he mean, we can't leave?"

"If we lose, we're stuck in the game forever," Rox_Ur_Sox explained.

Em3ra1d bit her lip. "That doesn't seem very fair . . . or legal."

Rox_Ur_Sox shrugged. "It was in the contract, apparently."

"I sure wish I remembered signing that thing."

D4rkHunter suddenly yelped and jumped back from the edge of the pier, his eyes wide. "There's something in the water."

The other three crowded around him and looked where he pointed. The waves below lapped around pillars caked with barnacles. But there was no other movement.

"I don't see anything," Em3ra1d said. The water was so dark it was almost black.

"It was there a second ago, I swear," said D4rkHunter.

"It was probably just a fish," E1_Kapitan said.

D4rkHunter looked doubtful. "Yeah, maybe . . ."

"What are we even supposed to be looking for?" Rox_Ur_Sox asked. "How do we defeat the Water Level?"

"The Game Runner never said," mumbled D4rkHunter as he eyed the water warily.

"C'mon," Rox_Ur_Sox said, "we should see if there's any useful stuff in the other shacks."

While the other three players explored every building on the half-circle pier, Em3ra1d studied her spell book, trying to memorize the spells and what they did. *I might be terrible at video games,* she thought, *but no one can cram for a test like I can.*

Eventually, the rest of the party returned.

"Nothing!" Rox_Ur_Sox said, throwing up her hands. "This is stupid. There's no loot and no Health potions."

"We'll have to monitor our Health and Power crystals carefully then," D4rkHunter said.

It was still twilight on the pier. The sun hadn't moved at all, and the sky hadn't grown any darker. Em3ra1d wondered if the game was designed that way. The only difference in their surroundings was that a fog was beginning to creep in.

"Look!" Em3ra1d pointed at a golden glow in the water.

"There's probably something in the water that we need to get," Rox_Ur_Sox said.

"But who's going to get it?" E1_Kapitan asked.

D4rkHunter cleared his throat nervously. "Guys, I think this first level is meant for me."

"What do you mean?" Em3ra1d asked.

"Remember how the Game Runner said that each level would test our deepest fears?"

"Yeah?"

D4rkHunter took a deep breath. "When I was a kid, I used to go to the ocean with my dads all the time. But one time, I went out swimming, got caught in a current, and almost drowned. I've been terrified of water ever since."

"That's crazy!" E1_Kapitan puffed up his cheeks and blew out a little puff of air. "I'd be scared too, if that had happened to me."

"How do you shower, Hunter?" asked Rox_Ur_Sox with a smirk.

D4rkHunter rolled his eyes. "Dude, Roxy, obviously I shower—I just don't like being in any water that goes above my waist." He looked down the ladder at the water. "This looks like it would definitely be over my head."

"We'll be right here if you need us," Em3ra1d said. "Don't worry. I volunteer as a lifeguard during the summer." She wondered if being a good swimmer in the real world made any difference in the virtual world.

D4rkHunter smiled weakly. "Thanks, Em." He turned around and descended the ladder. He gasped as the water sloshed past his waist.

"What is it?" E1_Kapitan asked.

"It's super cold!" D4rkHunter lowered himself into the water and paddled with one hand to keep afloat. He seemed reluctant to let go of his handhold on the ladder.

"You've got this, man!" E1_Kapitan gave him a thumbs-up and a cheesy smile.

D4rkHunter let go of the ladder and swam toward the golden glow. "There's definitely something here," he shouted, "but I'll have to dive to get it. It's on the bottom."

Em3ra1d thought she saw a flash of scales and something twisting just beneath the surface.

"What is *that*?" she asked, grabbing Rox_Ur_Sox's arm to get her attention.

The water rippled as the surface broke again.

"That's not a snake, is it?" Rox_Ur_Sox asked.

Em3ra1d swallowed. "I think they're *eels*."

"Hunter, look out!" Rox_Ur_Sox called.

D4rkHunter turned just in time to see an eel coming toward him. He thrashed in the water, trying to stay afloat as he reached for the quiver on his back. He grabbed an arrow and shoved it into the side of the eel. The arrow broke off at the shaft, but the eel hissed and slid back under the water.

"There's a ton more of those things!" D4rkHunter shouted, looking around frantically. "I'm gonna need some backup!"

"I can't reach them with my sword from here!" Rox_Ur_Sox said. "Warriors aren't really meant for long-range attacks."

E1_Kapitan aimed his Druid staff at the spot where the water was churning. Thorns launched from the end of his staff like darts and sliced into the water.

"Good idea, Kap!" D4rkHunter said. "I think you got some of them."

A weird clicking noise filled the air. "What is that?" Em3ra1d looked around for the source.

With a crackle of electricity, the water glowed neon purple.

D4rkHunter's avatar pixelated and vanished. Words floated in the sky above the spot:

D4RKHUNTER: DEATH 1 OF 3

CHAPTER 3

"*Electric* eels," Rox_Ur_Sox said in a horrified whisper.

It took a full minute for D4rkHunter to respawn. He appeared on the dock next to the rest of the party.

"What happened?" he asked.

"You died," E1_Kapitan said.

"Aw man! And it's only the first level."

"You must've lost all your Health before your red crystal could recharge," E1_Kapitan said.

"At least our Health and Power recharge fully when we respawn." D4rkHunter showed them that the red and blue crystals on his wristband were both glowing brightly.

"I think we'll have to get rid of those eels before you can get whatever is under the water," Rox_Ur_Sox said.

Something splashed in the water. D4rkHunter turned and fired an arrow at the spot. "I could shoot them from the dock, but I still need to dive for the object."

"No offense, but I'm a better swimmer," Em3ra1d said. "Why can't I get it?"

D4rkHunter shook his head. "If the whole point of these levels is to face our fears, then it really should be me. You guys will have to protect me while I get it."

"We're going to have an easier time fighting them if we're in the water. I can't see anything from up here." Rox_Ur_Sox headed for the ladder.

"Wait!" Em3ra1d said. "What if you get electrocuted like Hunter?"

"You've got to take chances in games, n00b," Rox_Ur_Sox said.

"Em's right," E1_Kapitan said. "Video games are all about timing. Let's just give it a second and see if there's some sort of pattern we can figure out."

They waited a moment, watching the water. Here and there, they caught glimpses of the eels. Then the clicking started.

"Count them!" Em3rald said.

They all counted silently until the clicking stopped and the water glowed purple for a moment.

"Five, right?" Em3rald asked.

The other players nodded.

"All right, so as soon as you hear that clicking," she instructed, "swim for the ladders as fast as you can. You'll have five clicks."

E1_Kapitan aimed his staff at the eels, and thick strands of seaweed shot out, wrapping around the eels and binding them. Three of the eels wriggled and vanished in a burst of dark green pixels. Rox_Ur_Sox slashed at a few more of them with her sword.

Em3rald jumped into the frigid water and swam away from the ladder with smooth, confident strokes. She still couldn't see much. Fog clung to the ocean's surface.

She took a deep breath and dived under. The visibility shouldn't have been much better, but when Em3ra1d opened her eyes, she found that she could see everything perfectly. The virtual water was dark green but crystal clear. And it didn't sting her eyes like real salt water.

The golden glow seemed to come from an object buried under a pile of white rocks.

No, Em3ra1d realized with a shudder, *a pile of bones.*

A dozen electric eels glided through the water. Every time D4rkHunter swam toward the glowing object, they blocked his path, nipping at his arms and legs.

Em3ra1d tried to think of a spell that would be useful. She had left her spell book on the pier since she didn't know if it would be waterproof. She could use *Lightning Bolt*.

But would that fry the water just like the eels?

There was a spell called *Fireball*.

Would that work underwater? Does magic in video games have to follow the laws of physics?

Virtual water or not, her lungs were beginning to burn from lack of oxygen. One of the eels rushed toward her.

Em3ra1d stuck out her hand. She spoke without opening her mouth, hoping that the mumbled spell would still work.

"*Acid!*"

A green cloud bubbled out from her hand. It surrounded the eel, and when it disappeared a moment later, the eel was gone.

Em3ra1d kicked her legs and shot up. Just as her head broke the surface and she gasped for air, the clicking started.

Click.

One, she thought, swimming as fast as she could toward the ladder.

Click.

Two. Out of the corner of her eye, she could see Rox_Ur_Sox pull herself up out the water.

Click.

Three. E1_Kapitan had made it too. *How did I let myself get this far out?*

Click.

Four. Even D4rkHunter had reached the pier. Em3ra1d was almost there. She grabbed desperately for the ladder and heaved.

Click.

Five.

Em3ra1d's foot had just cleared the water when the electricity sparked. She could feel the static and heat as the purple energy surged below her.

The water turned still and black again. Em3ra1d nearly sobbed with relief, her arms shaking as she clung to the ladder. She had always assumed people played video games for fun. And if there was one thing she wasn't having right now it was—

Em3ra1d screamed as an eel lunged from the water and bit her leg. She lost her grip on the ladder, tumbling back into the cold water.

The eels closed in around her, their gaping mouths filled with jagged teeth.

The world faded to black, but there were words written on the blackness:

```
EM3RALD_WITH_3NVY:
    DEATH 1 OF 3
```

CHAPTER 4

When Em3ra1d respawned on the dock, it felt like only one or two seconds had passed, but she remembered that it had taken sixty seconds for D4rkHunter to come back to life.

Em3ra1d tried to get her bearings. Rox_Ur_Sox had found a rowboat somewhere and had paddled out to the middle of the bay. She was leaning over the side, trying to hack at eels with her sword without tipping over the boat. E1_Kapitan was on the dock, sending more thorn darts shooting into the water from his staff.

Em3ra1d knew she would be more helpful in the water. She ran along the dock, jumped, and dove into the water, coming up next to Rox_Ur_Sox in her rowboat.

"Oh good, you're back," Rox_Ur_Sox said, rolling her eyes. "I don't know how we'd ever survive without your powerful Mage spells." She brought the hilt of her sword down on the nose of an eel that had come too close, and it disappeared. "I'm just glad I found this boat tied to the dock. Do you know how hard it is to tread water when you're weighed down with Warrior armor?"

Em3ra1d ducked under the water and pointed at the eels that had clustered around the boat.

"*Confusion!*" Once again, the spell seemed to work even when it was gurgled underwater. The eels started to drift slowly in circles, changing direction randomly. Some of them bumped into each other.

Em3ra1d popped above the water. "I think I confused them!" she called to Rox_Ur_Sox.

"I guess that helps? It would have been better if you could've just killed some." Rox_Ur_Sox slashed at another eel and it disappeared. "This does make them easier to hit, though."

Back underwater, Em3ra1d used another cloud of *Acid*. Her Power was very low from spellcasting, and multiple eel bites had drained her red Health crystal, but now there was only one eel left. And besides, she could see that D4rkHunter had almost uncovered the glowing object in the pile of bones.

The final eel darted through the water to attack D4rkHunter from behind. The clicking started again. One click. Two clicks. Three clicks.

Em3ra1d was torn between swimming for the ladder and helping D4rkHunter. The eels were the ones electrifying the water, so if they killed the last one . . .

She had just raised her hand to cast a spell when D4rkHunter spun around in the water, his cloak billowing out behind him. He had what looked like a leg bone in his hand. Four clicks. He smacked the eel in the face.

Five clicks.

Em3ra1d braced herself for the jolt of purple electricity, but at the last possible second, the eel pixelated and vanished.

D4rkHunter surfaced a moment after Em3ra1d_with_3nvy. He looked like he was having trouble, so Em3ra1d swam over and helped him to the ladder.

He flopped on the pier. He was breathing heavily, but he raised his hand up in triumph. He was holding a glowing golden key.

"I don't know about 'facing my fears,'" D4rkHunter said with a tight laugh. "If anything, I'm *more* freaked out by swimming now." He looked over his shoulder at the dark water. "Let's get out of here."

"Guess it's time for us to head for the next level," said El_Kapitan.

They stepped off the pier and headed toward the forest. Tall trees loomed above them—dark pines and gnarled oaks draped with moss. Thorn bushes and ferns filled the ground between the trees, so the only clear place to walk was a narrow path. The moon was full in the sky above the trees, but none of that light seemed to reach the path below. Em3ra1d couldn't see more than a few feet into the forest. Everything beyond that looked pitch-black, as though the game's programmers had forgotten to fill in the rest of the trees.

They found a large wooden treasure chest sitting at the edge of the forest.

D4rkHunter looked at the glowing key in his hand, shrugged, and knelt down in front of the chest. He inserted the key into the keyhole and turned it with a loud clunk. As they watched, the key turned to water in his hands. It maintained its shape for a moment and then splashed to the ground. The lid of the chest creaked open, revealing a bow and a quiver of arrows.

Now that she had something to compare them to, Em3ra1d realized how basic D4rkHunter's starting bow and arrows had been. Those had been made of plain wood. The new bow was made of glossy black wood and carved with runes. The arrows were tipped with polished black stone. The feathers at the end gleamed purple in the moonlight.

Words appeared above the chest:

SPARK BOW

"Awesome!" D4rkHunter said, examining his loot.

"All the best weapons have names," Rox_Ur_Sox said wistfully. "I can't wait to see what my new weapon will be called." She swept an arm toward the forest path. "Shall we?"

LEVEL 2

EARTH

CHAPTER 5

They entered the forest and were abruptly
swallowed up in the darkness. The forest
wasn't just *dark*. It seemed as though every last
bit of light had been sucked out of the world
in a split second. The change was so sudden
and overwhelming that Em3ra1d felt like she'd
been punched in the stomach.

The players stumbled along the path,
finding their way by touch. Em3ra1d kept one
hand on D4rkHunter's shoulder in front of
her and one hand out to the side. Her palm
brushed against rough tree bark, damp tangles
of moss, and thick, waxy leaves. Once, she
thought she felt fur. She gasped and jerked her

hand back, hoping she had imagined it.

"I literally can't see anything." Em3ra1d peered into the dark. She closed her eyes and opened them again, but there was no difference.

"Why don't you use your *Light* spell, Em?" E1_Kapitan asked.

Rox_Ur_Sox laughed harshly. "You saw what happened in the tutorial. We'd make it five feet before the spell fizzled out."

Em3ra1d felt her face grow hot and was glad no one could see her.

"It's not *that* dark," D4rkHunter protested.

"You're a Ranger," Rox_Ur_Sox said. "Rangers usually have great eyesight even in darkness."

"Good for him." E1_Kapitan's voice sounded strained.

"This is your level, isn't it, Kap?" Rox_Ur_Sox asked. "Are you afraid of the woods?"

"The dark?" Em3ra1d asked.

"Look, guys, I don't want to talk about it, okay?" E1_Kapitan said.

"Are you scared of squirrels?" D4rkHunter asked.

This seemed to break E1_Kapitan's unease for a moment. "*Squirrels?* For real, man? Why would I be scared of squirrels?"

There was a crackling sound, and a brilliant purple flare of light burst in the forest to their left.

They spun to look. D4rkHunter had fired an arrow from his new Spark Bow at a creature that crouched on a low branch above their heads.

In the light from the arrow's electricity, Em3ra1d could see that it was a squirrel, all right, but it was bigger and looked much meaner than any she had seen. It had oversized yellow eyes like an owl, and when it opened its mouth to shriek, Em3ra1d could see that it had multiple rows of shark-like teeth. The electricity coursed across its body for a few seconds, and then with a twitch the squirrel fell out of the tree. It pixelated and vanished, but the smell of burnt hair lingered.

Right before the light from the arrow went out, Em3ra1d saw the glowing green circles of countless eyes in the trees surrounding them.

And then the light was gone, and Em3rald felt blinder than before, like after a camera flash in a dark room. Purple afterimages splotched her vision as her eyes tried to readjust to the dark.

Answering shrieks and rasping barks echoed in the dark forest all around them. Branches rustled, and there was a sound of claws scrabbling on bark.

Em3rald yelped in surprise as a heavy weight landed on her shoulders, sharp claws scratching and tangling in her hair. Pain tingled across her scalp, and she saw her red Health crystal dim.

An arrow streaked out of the darkness like a lightning bolt, missing her by inches but knocking the squirrel off her back. In the light from the arrow, Em3rald could see the squirrels diving at them from all directions.

E1_Kapitan knocked one away with his staff. Another squirrel jumped at Rox_Ur_Sox from above. She swung her shield over her head to deflect the attack and the squirrel bounced off and fell to the ground, chittering angrily.

D4rkHunter continued to fire his electric arrows, picking off squirrels one by one. The arrows lit up the night, turning the dark into twisting nightmarish shadows filled with glowing eyes and gleaming teeth. Each time the arrows flared, the party had a brief moment where they could see the monstrous squirrels that were attacking them. But the light would soon fade and leave them blind again.

Em3ra1d flipped through her spell book desperately during the times the arrows lit up the dark forest and gave her enough light to read by. She didn't dare use the *Light* spell again after how badly it had failed during the tutorial. She needed something *good*, something to prove that she was useful. Why were there so many spells?

Finally, she found it. She aimed her hand at the squirrels, which were currently swarming Rox_Ur_Sox.

"*Fireball!*" A ball of green flames shot from her hand and swept over the squirrels. When the flame flickered away, all of the squirrels had vanished, either defeated or scared off into the woods.

I did it! Em3ra1d thought excitedly. Maybe she could be a useful party member after all—

"You. Are. Such. An. IDIOT!" Rox_Ur_Sox's voice growled from the darkness.

Em3ra1d's confidence vanished as quickly as it had come. "Why? We beat them!"

"Couple of notes, n00b." Rox_Ur_Sox sounded like she was trying to keep her temper. "First of all, it's called 'friendly fire' when you attack the enemy and end up hurting your own party members."

In the dark, Em3ra1d_with_3nvy saw a faint red glow and realized it was Rox_Ur_Sox's Health crystal. The *Fireball* spell had drained almost all of it.

Em3ra1d felt her stomach drop. "I'm sorry—"

"Chill, Roxy," E1_Kapitan said. "Your Health will recharge soon."

"Second," Rox_Ur_Sox continued, ignoring him, "you never want to waste a high-level spell on low-level enemies."

Em3ra1d looked down at her blue Power crystal. It was as depleted as Rox_Ur_Sox's red Health crystal. She would have to wait for her Power to recharge before she could cast any sort of useful spell again.

"Wait," she said, "what do you mean 'low-level'? Wasn't that the enemy we were supposed to defeat for the Earth Level?"

"Those little guys were too easy, Em," D4rkHunter explained quietly. "They were just a distraction."

Em3ra1d's heart beat faster. "A distraction from what?"

Another lightning arrow flared from D4rkHunter's Spark Bow just in time to illuminate a giant bear as it lumbered from the shadows. It was already taller than them at the shoulder when it was on all four legs. Em3ra1d didn't want to think about how tall it would be if it stood on its hind legs. Two long, dagger-shaped teeth jutted from its mouth, each one as thick as her arm. A *saber-toothed* bear. The lightning from the arrow made its fur bristle with static but didn't seem to do as much damage as it did to the squirrels.

The saber-toothed bear narrowed its huge green eyes and snarled. Its breath smelled like rotting meat.

In one quick motion, its paw darted out and swatted Rox_Ur_Sox.

Her Health crystal never had a chance to recharge.

```
ROX_UR_SOX: DEATH 1 OF 3
```

CHAPTER 6

Em3ra1d knew it would only be a minute until Rox_Ur_Sox respawned. But the saber-toothed bear growled, a deep rumbling bass that vibrated her bones, and sixty seconds felt like a lifetime.

"Keep your head in the game, Em!" D4rkHunter called. "Everyone makes mistakes."

He shot a couple of arrows at the beast, but it just wasn't enough. The saber-toothed bear lunged at D4rkHunter. Em3ra1d saw a flash of giant, razor-sharp teeth, and then D4rkHunter's avatar pixelated and vanished.

D4RKHUNTER: DEATH 2 OF 3

The light from the arrow went out, plunging them once more into darkness. Em3ra1d braced herself for the attack, but it never came. She hardly dared to breathe.

"Why isn't it attacking us, Kap?" she asked, her voice barely above a whisper.

"I think it's hunting us. For fun," E1_Kapitan replied in a shaky voice.

He sounded close, so Em3ra1d reached out, found his hand, and squeezed it reassuringly. It was clammy and trembling.

"What do we do now?" he asked. "Can you use a spell?"

Em3ra1d checked her Power. It was recharging slowly, but the crystal was still a very faint blue. "I don't have enough Power yet for a high-level spell." They couldn't afford to wait for her Power to recharge or for D4rkHunter and Rox_Ur_Sox to respawn. The saber-toothed bear had to be lurking nearby.

The silence that pressed in on them was almost worse than the darkness. There were no insect noises, no breezes to stir the leaves. Just the sound of their shallow breathing and a dull thudding sound that might have been their own heartbeats. Em3rald froze as a twig snapped in the forest to her right.

"I wish we had night vision like Hunter," E1_Kapitan muttered.

She suddenly thought of the large eyes on both the squirrels and the saber-toothed bear. She knew from last year's biology class that nocturnal animals could see in the dark because they had big eyes that let in more light. She had just enough Power for *that*.

A low growl came from the darkness in front of her and grew into a roar. She had no way of knowing where exactly the saber-toothed bear was, but she aimed her hand at what she hoped was the direction of its eyes and screamed, "*Light!*"

She didn't know if it was because she said it like she meant it this time, or if she was just getting better at magic, but this time there was no feeble light like in the tutorial. Instead a large sphere of light blazed like a miniature sun in the air in front of her.

The saber-toothed bear crashed out of the trees, and her spell surprised it in mid-charge.

Em3ra1d barely dodged out of the way as the bear bellowed and flopped heavily to the ground, its eyes shut in pain.

E1_Kapitan aimed his staff at the blinded saber-toothed bear. Vines shot out of the staff—thick rope-like vines with sharp thorns. They coiled around the saber-toothed bear's legs like snakes, then crawled up, winding around its body, binding it in place. The vines twisted and grew until Em3ra1d couldn't even see the saber-toothed bear underneath the choking layer of the leaves and thorns.

The creature growled one last time, and then there was silence. The vines fell limply to the ground. The saber-toothed bear had vanished.

Rox_Ur_Sox respawned a second later. "Yay, you defeated it," she said in a flat voice.

D4rkHunter respawned next to her. "Nice! Good job, guys!"

E1_Kapitan bent down to examine the pile of vines. He held up a shining gold key and grinned.

CHAPTER 7

Rox_Ur_Sox walked up to Em3ra1d, her face furious. "Were you *trying* to get me killed?"

Em3ra1d was forced to take a step back. "No, of course not." She folded her arms across her chest. "Look, I didn't even want to be here in the first place!"

"Well, you're here now," Rox_Ur_Sox said, "and the only way out of here is to win."

"I'm trying to be a better player—"

"Try *harder*!" Rox_Ur_Sox put her hands on her hips.

"You *are* getting better, Em," E1_Kapitan said. "I never could have defeated the Earth Level without you."

Em3ra1d felt a surge of pride.

"Yeah, go easy on her, Roxy," D4rkHunter called over his shoulder as he searched the ground for arrows he could reuse. "It's her first time playing a game like this."

"I don't know how you can be so sympathetic, Hunter," Rox_Ur_Sox snapped. "You've died twice in the first two levels. One more time and you're out for the count."

"But those weren't my fault!" Em3ra1d protested.

"Not directly." Rox_Ur_Sox pursed her lips angrily. "But this would be a whole lot easier if we had a Mage who knew what she was doing."

"Aw, c'mon Roxy," El_Kapitan said with a sly smile. "You can't tell me a pro-gamer like you wants things to be *easy*?"

Rox_Ur_Sox rolled her eyes, but she managed a small smile. "Fine. Maybe I *do* love a challenge." A scowl quickly replaced her smile when she looked at Em3ra1d. "But you're still on notice, n00b." She strode off down the path out of the forest.

The rest of the party followed her.

"So, what *was* your fear, Kap?" D4rkHunter asked. "And don't tell me it was saber-toothed bears."

"Fine," E1_Kapitan said. "I went on a camping trip last summer with my *abuela* and my mom and my cousins. I had to leave the tent in the middle of the night to use the bathroom. And one of my cousins thought it would be hilarious to leap out of the woods at me wearing a Halloween mask." He smiled sheepishly.

"You gotta love family bonding," D4rkHunter said, laughing.

The light from Em3ra1d's spell began to fade as her Power drained, so the party hurried to the edge of the forest.

"Look, there's the chest!" E1_Kapitan ran over and unlocked it with his key. This time the key crumbled away into dirt. The staff inside seemed to be made of shadows and swirling gray smoke. From certain angles, it was almost entirely see-through. It didn't look like a solid, physical object, but E1_Kapitan was able to lift it out of the chest.

The message above the chest read:

SHADOW STAFF

E1_Kapitan raised the staff slightly and then brought it down with a soft thud. His avatar flickered and disappeared. If Em3ra1d looked closely, she could see a shimmery patch of air and a faint silver outline where he stood, but he was almost completely invisible. They heard another thump and he reappeared.

"That's so cool!" D4rkHunter exclaimed.

E1_Kapitan grinned proudly.

Rox_Ur_Sox sighed. "I'm happy for you guys, but I think it's a little unfair that you get sweet leveled-up weapons and I'm still stuck with my starter shield and sword."

Em3ra1d hadn't known enough about video game weapons to notice before, but compared to the new weapons that E1_Kapitan and D4rkHunter had received, Rox_Ur_Sox's weapons were plain and boring. The sword even looked a little rusty.

She looked at her spell book. It was tattered and musty and the leather cover was peeling. Maybe when she beat her level, she would get a gorgeous hardcover book, bound with midnight blue leather and gold embossed lettering. She realized she hadn't thought about what fear she would have to face in her level. She just hoped it wouldn't be—

"Hey, let's go already," Rox_Ur_Sox said.

LEVEL 3

FIRE

CHAPTER 8

They pushed past the last bunch of trees and came out onto an open plain of jagged, black rock. The ground sloped up to the smoking mountain peak they had seen from the pier. The sky was covered in dark clouds, lit red from beneath. As the group watched, a fountain of lava spewed from the mountaintop. The ground shook.

"I really hope this level doesn't involve climbing an erupting volcano," Rox_Ur_Sox said. "Because I'm not a huge fan of heat. Or fiery volcanic death."

Lava flowed down the mountain in bright red rivers and webs of molten gold. Even at this distance, the air shimmered with heat. Ash and rocks began to rain down on their heads, and their red Health crystals dimmed slightly.

"We're losing Health!" Rox_Ur_Sox deflected another shower of burning rocks with her shield. "We need to find cover."

Em3ra1d scanned the area. Everything was rock, ash, and lava, but she thought she could make out a path. She spotted a cave on the side of the volcano, shielded from lava flows by a stone overhang.

"I think we're supposed to go that way!" she shouted over the roar of the eruption.

They ran for the cave, dodging chunks of rock and flaming stone. The heat grew even worse the closer they got. Em3ra1d was already drenched with sweat. Beads of it ran down her back and stung her eyes.

She really hoped she was right about the cave. *Just a little farther.* She could feel the heat of the ground through her boots. Her red Health crystal was getting dimmer and dimmer from the choking ash and intense heat.

"Look out!" someone called, but Em3ra1d had already seen the giant lava flow cascading down the mountain, heading toward them like a fiery tidal wave.

"Everyone into the cave!" Rox_Ur_Sox shouted.

They barely made it in time. El_Kapitan dove in at the last moment. Lava spilled over the stone overhang, creating a molten curtain that trapped them in the cave.

The heat was unbearable. Em3ra1d could feel her skin scorching and her lungs burning as she drew in a breath of superheated air and ash. The red glow from their Health crystals grew weaker as the red glow of the lava grew brighter.

"What—do—we—do?" Rox_Ur_Sox croaked. "Going to—pass out." She started coughing and choking, unable to get a breath.

D4rkHunter's face was nearly as red as Rox_Ur_Sox's armor.

Em3ra1d scanned the back of the cave, but her vision swam, and she couldn't see anything that looked like a door. Her vision darkened at the corners. She dropped her spell book as she doubled over, coughing.

The book fell open to a specific page, as if by magic. *It probably was magic,* thought Em3rald. A spell caught her eyes. It had to work. *Please.*

E1_Kapitan sank to his knees, and D4rkHunter toppled over. Dust and ash filled the small space, and lava still blocked the way out.

Em3rald weakly aimed her hand over all of them. She tried to say the spell, but nothing came out but more coughs.

"*Flame Guard,*" she wheezed, hoping it would be enough.

Suddenly she could breathe again. She inhaled deeply. The air was still hot, but it wasn't any worse than summer in Florida. Her red Health crystal began to recharge.

"Is everyone okay?" D4rkHunter asked, staggering to his feet. "Any deaths?"

"We're all still here," E1_Kapitan said between gulps of fresh air. "Good thinking with that spell, Em."

"Yeah, thanks," Rox_Ur_Sox said without looking at her.

Em3ra1d held up her hand. It was covered with a thin film that shimmered with rainbow patterns like a soap bubble. She could see the same sheen on the other players. It was the *Flame Guard* spell—an actual layer of protection on their skin.

"We really need to be more careful," El_Kapitan reminded them as everyone panted to catch their breath. "We almost all died at once. Remember, the Game Runner said that means 'game over' for all of us."

D4rkHunter nodded. "Well, now that we can actually breathe, how do we get out of here?"

Em3ra1d checked the back of the cave. She thought she had seen something before she almost passed out. Sure enough, there was a narrow tunnel close to the ground. As she stuck her hand in, lights in the sides of the tunnel came to life and filled it with a dim yellow glow. There was barely room to squeeze through. They would have to crawl on their bellies.

"I think we're supposed to go through here," she said.

E1_Kapitan raised an eyebrow when he saw how small it was, but then he shrugged. "Eh, whatever, at least it's not dark."

"You've got to be kidding me," said Rox_Ur_Sox, her eyes wide. "There's no way we'll fit." Her voice shook slightly.

E1_Kapitan grinned. "Wait, don't tell me our fearless Warrior is scared of the tunnel. Is this your level, Roxy?"

"I guess it must be." Rox_Ur_Sox frowned. "I just don't like small, enclosed places." She peered into the tunnel. "Tiny, cramped, claustrophobic places where I could get stuck and never get out." She gulped.

D4rkHunter walked over to her. "Why are you scared of—?"

"There's no horror story or bad childhood memory behind it," Rox_Ur_Sox snapped. "It just freaks me out. It's a perfectly reasonable thing to be scared of."

He held up his hands. "Fair enough. But I think it's the only way for us to move forward.

There's still lava blocking the mouth of the cave. And I doubt even this *Flame Guard* spell would protect us from that."

"Speaking of *Flame Guard*," Em3ra1d said, "this spell is slowly draining my Power. I don't want to use up it all up before we defeat this level, so we should probably hurry."

D4rkHunter crawled into the tunnel first. After a while, he yelled back to them. "I can't see the end, but it's clear so far. Follow me in."

"I might as well get it over with," Rox_Ur_Sox said with a grimace. "If I wait to go last, I'll psych myself out and won't be able to do it. And then you'll have to go on without me."

"No one's leaving you, Roxy," E1_Kapitan said. "Your shield, on the other hand . . ."

"What?" Rox_Ur_Sox said sharply, clutching her shield to her chest. "I can't leave my shield!"

"You'll still have your sword," E1_Kapitan reasoned. "But that shield is wider than the tunnel. Unless it folds up, there's no way it's going to fit through."

Rox_Ur_Sox looked at Em3ra1d. "I don't suppose you have a spell for folding up shields?"

Em3ra1d shook her head.

"Are you guys coming or not?" D4rkHunter's muffled voice echoed back down the tunnel.

Rox_Ur_Sox sighed. "Ready or not," she called back half-heartedly before setting her shield against the cave wall. Then she got down on her belly in an army crawl. She held her sword awkwardly in one hand, aimed point first down the tunnel.

"You should just strap your sword across your back," E1_Kapitan called to her.

"I'm not going to be defenseless if I run into something in this creepy tunnel," they heard her snap back.

Em3ra1d went next. *Rox_Ur_Sox is right about this tunnel being creepy,* she thought as she crawled along. The ground quaked with the force of the erupting volcano above them. The lights flickered and dirt shook free from the ceiling. Once or twice, the tunnel narrowed until she could hardly move. She had to dig in with her toes to push herself forward, inch by inch.

She thought she could hear Rox_Ur_Sox muttering angrily to herself from somewhere up ahead.

The tunnel seemed to go on forever, and Em3rald was grateful when she finally reached the end. She wriggled out of the tunnel and stood up slowly. She tried to massage the kinks out of her sore muscles. It felt like they had been crawling for hours. E1_Kapitan exited the tunnel behind her.

Rox_Ur_Sox brushed dirt off her armor. Sweat poured down her face, her forehead crinkled with anxiety.

"It's not as much fun when it's your own fear you have to face, is it?" D4rkHunter said, poking her gently in the arm.

"Whatever," Rox_Ur_Sox said grumpily, redoing her ponytail. "Let's just get this level over with. At least it's less claustrophobic now."

Em3rald examined their surroundings. They were in a large cavern. Pools of lava bubbled here and there, giving the room a red glow. "I need to save Power, guys," Em3ra1d explained as she lowered the *Flame Guard* spell. The air was still hot, but it was clear.

Stalactites and stalagmites sprouted from the ceiling and floor of the cavern. Em3ra1d looked up. The cavern seemed to rise to a peak at the top. How could the volcano be erupting *outside* if it was hollow *inside*? She shook her head, reminding herself that it was a video game. Things didn't have to make real-world sense.

An ear-splitting screech echoed in the cavern high above them. A massive fiery bird circled overhead. Its feathers were the color of molten lava—shades of crimson, orange, and gold.

Em3ra1d gasped. "Is that a *phoenix*?"

The phoenix swooped down to attack Rox_Ur_Sox. She raised her arm to fend it off, but at the last second, she seemed to remember that she no longer had a shield for defense. With a yell, she dove to the side in a half somersault, the talons scraping her shoulder. She brought up her sword as she landed and slashed at the phoenix. A shower of red feathers floated down around her.

E1_Kapitan used his staff to shoot thorn darts at the phoenix. It squawked and reared back as they hit, but it wasn't enough damage. The phoenix flew at him, talons outstretched, but E1_Kapitan struck the ground with his Shadow Staff and turned invisible. The phoenix screeched in frustration as more thorn darts shot out of nowhere.

E1_Kapitan reappeared suddenly, his eyes wide. Em3ra1d could see from the dull blue crystal on his wristband that his Power had run out. The phoenix dug its talons into E1_Kapitan's leather jacket. Before the rest of them could react, the phoenix half-dragged, half-threw E1_Kapitan into one of the lava pools. He pixelated instantly.

EL_KAPITAN: DEATH 1 OF 3

The phoenix circled over their heads and screeched again. It pulled in its wings and dive-bombed Em3ra1d.

Em3ra1d_with_3nvy yelled the first spell that came into her head.

"*Fireball!*"

None of the other players are nearby to take friendly fire, she reasoned. *And it's okay to use a high-powered spell on a high-level enemy.*

The plume of green Mage flame hit the phoenix square in the face.

It didn't damage the phoenix at all.

She thought she heard Rox_Ur_Sox yell. "*Fire* Level, n00b! FIRE!"

Of course, thought Em3ra1d as the phoenix's talons hit her in the chest and knocked her to the ground. Flames glowed deep in its throat like a furnace as it opened its beak wide. *You can't fight fire with fire.*

EM3RALD_WITH_3NVY:
DEATH 2 OF 3

CHAPTER 9

When Em3ra1d respawned, it was right in the thick of the battle. She felt like things were moving in slow motion around her. E1_Kapitan had respawned behind a pile of rocks, but he seemed to have trouble getting around them without putting himself right in the phoenix's way. The phoenix was attacking Rox_Ur_Sox, its giant wings churning the air around them. Fire shot from its mouth as if it were a dragon.

Em3ra1d dove in front of Rox_Ur_Sox and threw up her hand. *"Ice Wall!"*

A sheet of ice flew up in front of them like a force field. The phoenix's flame hit the wall instead of Rox_Ur_Sox.

The ice melted in seconds. A cloud of hot steam surrounded them, blocking them from the phoenix's view for several moments. Rox_Ur_Sox grabbed Em3rald's hand and they ducked behind a stalagmite on the other side of the cave. The phoenix shrieked, unable to find any of them in the thick fog.

"That was so cool!" Rox_Ur_Sox whispered excitedly. "You just came out of nowhere, like BAM." Then she seemed to remember she was talking to Em3rald. She blushed and looked away. "Thanks for saving me, n00b. I guess."

"How are we going to defeat this thing?" Em3rald asked as D4rkHunter scurried over to join them.

"I have an idea," he said and leaned in to explain it to them.

As the steam cloud began to lift, the players put D4rkHunter's plan into action. Rox_Ur_Sox ran into the middle of the cavern. "Come and get me, you giant fire turkey!" she yelled. She pounded her chest, the hilt of her sword clanging loudly on her armor.

The phoenix didn't need much persuading. It screeched and swooped down toward Rox_Ur_Sox.

"Now!" Rox_Ur_Sox shouted.

D4rkHunter leapt up on a rock and shot two arrows, one right after the other, into a large stalactite on the ceiling. The arrows soared through the air, and when they hit the base of the stalactite, the electric jolt was explosive. The whole cavern shook and rocks rained down from the ceiling. Em3rald hoped it would be enough. With a loud crack, the stalactite came loose, coming down with a thunderous crash. D4rkHunter ran for cover, but Rox_Ur_Sox was still right underneath the falling stalactite and would never be able to get out of the way in time.

"*Teleport!*" Em3rald yelled. She appeared right next to Rox_Ur_Sox and grabbed her arm. A split second later, the two of them reappeared at a safe distance. A wave of dust and gravel blew over them as the stalactite crashed down right where Rox_Ur_Sox had been a second ago.

"Okay, okay," Rox_Ur_Sox said. "Now you're just showing off."

"I believe that's twice that the n00b has saved your life during the Fire Level," E1_Kapitan reminded her with an amused grin when he joined them.

"Just because I don't know all the rules of the game doesn't mean I can't figure it out," Em3ra1d pointed out. "And the only way I'm going to learn is by taking big risks and learning from my mistakes."

"Well, if your mistakes get me killed and your successes save my life, I suppose that balances out." Rox_Ur_Sox rolled her eyes, but Em3ra1d thought she saw her mouth twitch into something like a smile.

When the dust cleared, they could see that not only the stalactite but also half of the cavern ceiling had collapsed on the phoenix.

Rox_Ur_Sox edged closer to the pile of rubble, her sword at the ready. "That must have finished it, right? Where's my key?"

The pile of rubble suddenly burst into flames. As they watched, the rocks melted into molten lava, streaming down the pile and running into the lava pools around the cavern. Em3ra1d threw up the *Flame Guard* spell, which used the last of her Power.

But nothing happened. The bonfire burned itself out, and soon there was only a pile of ash where the rocks had been. There was no sign of the phoenix.

Then the pile of ashes began to glow and shift. Something was buried underneath.

"Oh no," Em3ra1d said. "It's rising from the ashes!"

"Isn't that what phoenixes are supposed to do?" D4rkHunter asked.

"Yeah, but does this mean we have to fight it again?" Rox_Ur_Sox asked. "My Health hasn't recharged yet. And after all that fancy spell work, I'm sure Em's Power is shot."

Em3ra1d pretended to check her blue Power crystal, but she already knew that it was completely empty. She just used the action to hide the smile that crept over her face when she realized that Rox_Ur_Sox had called her "Em" and not "n00b" for the first time.

"Maybe it's a glitch?" El_Kapitan said. "I mean, that's why L33T C0RP needs beta testers, right?"

D4rkHunter sighed and notched an arrow to his bow. "Here we go again."

Ashes flew into the air with a familiar screech and a blaze of golden feathers.

Then they noticed how much smaller the phoenix was. It still had wicked-looking talons and a sharp beak underneath its wild golden eyes, but it barely came up to Em3ra1d's waist.

It landed in the pile of ashes and stared at them, cocking its head to one side.

"What are we supposed to do?" Rox_Ur_Sox asked, not daring to speak above a whisper.

The phoenix whipped its head around to stare at her, and Em3ra1d saw Rox_Ur_Sox fighting the urge to back away from its fierce gaze.

Rox_Ur_Sox knelt and held out her hand to the phoenix.

"What are you doing?" D4rkHunter hissed.

"Shut up, I don't know if this will work," Rox_Ur_Sox said through gritted teeth.

The phoenix bent its head toward her hand, and opened its beak. Fire shot out, surrounding Rox_Ur_Sox's hand with flames.

Em3rald stifled a gasp. El_Kapitan had to restrain D4rkHunter from rushing forward. Rox_Ur_Sox didn't seem to be in any pain, though her wide eyes reflected the firelight.

The flame disappeared. With a final screech, the phoenix flew off into the shadows at the very top of the cavern and disappeared from view. The cavern was silent except for the glop of bubbling lava in the pools and the ragged breathing of the players.

In Rox_Ur_Sox's hand, where the phoenix fire had touched it, lay a golden key.

They found Rox_Ur_Sox's chest at the far end of the cavern, next to a stone door. When she inserted the golden key, nothing happened at first. Then the key began to glow redder and redder. Drops of melted gold hissed as they hit the cavern floor, and soon the key was just a puddle of liquid metal. The chest opened.

VOLCANIC WAR HAMMER

When Rox_Ur_Sox picked up the giant hammer, she had to grip the long handle with two hands. The hammer's head was charcoal black with deep cracks of glowing red and orange, as though a thin, black crust had formed over a molten lava core.

"*Much* better." With a mischievous grin, Rox_Ur_Sox hoisted the war hammer up so she could carry it over one shoulder. She looked happier than she had during the entire game so far.

They opened the door next to the chest. A flight of stairs spiraled up, lit by torches every few feet.

They began to climb.

And climb.

And climb.

Em3rald's feet dragged and kept catching on the edge of the steps, threatening to trip her. From time to time, El_Kapitan would stop, slouch against the wall, and sigh dramatically. Even D4rkHunter was breathing heavily.

"We must be near the top of the mountain by now," Rox_Ur_Sox panted from several stairs below them. "You have no idea how heavy a full suit of armor and giant war hammer are."

By the time they had reached the top of the stairs, everyone's Health and Power crystals had recharged fully from the battle with the phoenix.

Em3ra1d looked at the stone door on the other end of the landing, and with a sinking feeling in the pit of her stomach, she realized that what lay behind the door had to be *her* level. She'd been so caught up in the action and excitement of the last level that for a moment she had completely forgotten that she would have to face her fears, just like everyone else. D4rkHunter had completed the Water Level, E1_Kapitan had defeated the Earth Level, and Rox_Ur_Sox had beaten the Fire Level. That just left . . . the Air Level.

Em3ra1d thought of all the stairs they had climbed. *Air Level.* She knew what she would have to face, and the thought made her queasy.

Rox_Ur_Sox flung open the door. "Let's do this!"

A cold wind gusted into the chamber. They stepped outside.

LEVEL 4

AIR

CHAPTER 10

After the dark of the forest and the lava caves, the players squinted and blinked in the sunlight of a cloudless sky. They were at the top of a snowcapped mountain peak, with no volcano in sight. Snow-covered mountains stretched away from them in all directions. Still sweaty from the Fire Level, the players shivered in the brisk wind.

D4rkHunter pointed across an impossibly deep chasm to another mountain peak. "I think we're supposed to go there," he said.

Em3ra1d could see a dark shadow on the mountainside that looked to be some sort of cave. A long and narrow stone bridge crossed the vast space without any support pillars. There were no handrails or guide ropes either.

It was the only way across.

A strong wind battered them and Em3ra1d's Mage cloak billowed out behind her. She looked at the cave in the distance and then at the bridge again. It was barely wide enough for two people to walk across at the same time.

She looked down into the chasm beneath the bridge. She couldn't see the bottom. She was intensely aware of the empty space, of the nothingness that stood between her at this dizzying height and the ground far below.

Her heart thrashed against her rib cage, and the breath snagged in her throat. She breathed in wheezing, panicked gasps, her mind clouding with terror.

She heard everyone's voices as if from a long way off.

"Em? What's happening?" D4rkHunter asked.

"What's wrong with her?" Rox_Ur_Sox asked. "Is she okay?"

Em3ra1d shook violently. She couldn't stop gasping for air long enough to answer, even if her brain had been able to string together clear thoughts. Her heart felt like it was trying to crawl right out of her skin. Every muscle was painfully tight.

"I think she's having a panic attack," she heard E1_Kapitan explain to the others. He knelt down beside her but continued to give her some space. "Look, Em, I'm not going to tell you to calm down, but I want to you to take some deep breaths for me, okay?"

Em3ra1d managed to nod. She attempted a couple of long, shaky breaths.

"Good," E1_Kapitan said. "We don't have to start the level until you're absolutely ready. Until then, just remember that we're here for you."

"We're so close to the end," D4rkHunter added. "Just one more level and the Boss Battle, and then we can get out of here. We're going to help you get through this, Em."

Even Rox_Ur_Sox chimed in. "You're pretty decent for a n00b, I guess," she said with a small smirk, kneeling in front of Em3rald. "And the world could always use more girl gamers."

Em3rald felt a small laugh cut through her panic, and her muscles relaxed slightly. Her chest gradually loosened, and she began to breathe more easily. "Thanks, guys," she said with a weak smile.

Rox_Ur_Sox helped Em3rald to her feet. "I know you can do this. At the rate you're picking this stuff up, you'll be a better gamer than me before you know it."

Em3rald raised an eyebrow. "Seriously?"

Rox_Ur_Sox jabbed a thumb over her shoulder at E1_Kapitan and D4rkHunter. "Or at least better than those guys," she said in a stage whisper. She dodged a playful shoulder punch from E1_Kapitan as D4rkHunter shouted, "Hey!"

Rox_Ur_Sox shrugged, unapologetic, and Em3rald laughed again with the others.

"Are we good to go?" D4rkHunter asked. "Just remind yourself that it's only a video game."

"Yeah, but I've already died twice," Em3ra1d said. "If I die a third time, I'll be trapped here forever. So it's almost as bad as a *real* bottomless pit, except my avatar would pixelate before I splatted at the bottom . . . I hope."

"We'll go first, and you can crawl," El_Kapitan said. "No judgment if you crawl. We'll handle fighting whatever monster shows up. You can attack it with spells from your safe crawling position, with a nice low center of gravity."

Em3ra1d appreciated his light-hearted approach, but she knew that she had no choice in the matter. They could stand on this ledge in the freezing cold as long as they liked, but that would never win them the game. There was only one way forward, just like she had told Rox_Ur_Sox back in the Fire Level. If the other three players could face their fears, then so could she.

They started across. The bridge was a little wider than it had looked, but not by much. Em3ra1d didn't crawl, but she stayed in the exact center of the bridge, her spell book tucked in her robe and her hands out for balance. The wind whistled around her.

At first, Em3ra1d had been thankful that it was a solid stone bridge. She had always hated the idea of those swaying bridges in action movies, with fraying ropes and gaps between the boards. But at least those bridges had some sort of handrails. Em3ra1d would give anything now for a bridge with handrails.

She had the feeling that if she even looked at the edges of the bridge too long, she would somehow be pulled over the side. She reminded herself that she had about two feet of space on either side of her and focused on taking deep, even breaths. They were halfway there.

A rumbling sound like thunder filled the air. The wind picked up, howling around them. Boulders broke loose from the mountains on either side of the chasm and started swirling together in a vortex.

The floating rocks came together to form a huge shape—some sort of giant, with a head and arms attached to its bulky torso and legs that stretched down into the chasm below the bridge.

CHAPTER 11

The air giant brought down its fist, hitting
the bridge with a boom that echoed off the
mountainsides. The whole bridge shook, and
a huge chunk broke off and tumbled into the
chasm. The air giant roared, and it sounded
like a freight train.

"How are we supposed to fight that thing?"
Rox_Ur_Sox yelled. "It's huge!"

"This is my level, guys." Em3ra1d tried to
keep her voice from shaking. "You just focus
on staying alive, and I'll try to find some way
to defeat the monster." She had no idea how
she was going to do that.

Dust whirlwinds appeared at either end

of the bridge and spun toward them. The miniature dirt tornadoes might have been small in comparison to the air giant, but they were still as wide as the bridge. Em3ra1d threw herself flat on the bridge and the whirlwinds blew over her. Dust swirled around her and drained some of her Health crystal, but she stayed on the bridge. The other players did the same until the whirlwinds had passed.

D4rkHunter shot a few of his electric shock arrows at the air giant. Two passed harmlessly through the air in between the rocks that made up the giant's body, but the third one struck stone. A part of the air giant's arm exploded like the stalactite had in the lava cave.

The next time the air giant pounded the bridge with his fist, Rox_Ur_Sox ran up and struck it with her Volcanic War Hammer. As the blow landed, the head of the war hammer flared white-hot and part of the air giant's fist melted instantly, bursting into a shower of sparks and molten rock. The air giant made a noise that might have been a yell or might have been a hurricane.

It hit Rox_Ur_Sox and sent her flying. She landed on her back on the bridge, catching herself right before she rolled over the edge. But Em3ra1d could see that her red Health crystal was dangerously dim. Em3ra1d knew they had to be careful with their remaining lives if they wanted to beat the game. E1_Kapitan and Rox_Ur_Sox each had two lives left, but she and D4rkHunter were down to one life apiece. *Three strikes, you're out*, she remembered the Game Runner saying.

E1_Kapitan had seen Rox_Ur_Sox take damage too, and he did his best to distract the air giant until her Health crystal had a chance to recharge. He aimed his Shadow Staff at the air giant's chest. At first it looked like nothing had happened, but then the rock began to fracture. Roots exploded from inside the rock, like a tree growing through a crack in the pavement. The air giant staggered back, then brought its fist down on the bridge, roaring angrily.

E1_Kapitan dodged out of the way of the fist itself, but the vibration from the impact shook the bridge and he lost his balance. With a shout, he tumbled off the bridge into the chasm.

Reacting on instinct before her fear of heights could kick in, Em3ra1d grabbed for El_Kapitan's arm. She actually managed to hold him for a second before he slipped from her grasp with a shoulder-wrenching jerk.

El_Kapitan aimed his staff at the bridge as he dropped. Vines shot out from his staff and wrapped around the bridge. He stopped falling. Then the vines retracted back into the staff, pulling El_Kapitan back up and onto the bridge.

"That was close!" he said to Em3ra1d.

A dust whirlwind appeared behind him suddenly.

"Kap, look out!" she yelled, but it was too late for him to duck. She watched, horrified, as the dust whirlwind sucked up El_Kapitan.

EL_KAPITAN: DEATH 2 OF 3

CHAPTER 12

The whirlwind continued to spin toward
her, and Em3ra1d threw herself down on her
stomach again until it had passed over. She
tried not to look over the side of the bridge at
the gaping space beneath them, but then she
thought she saw something glint in the sunlight.

There it is again!

Em3ra1d realized it was her key. It was
hanging on a rope underneath the bridge, and
whenever the wind blew, it swung out into
view. The rope was too far away to reach, and
there was no way to climb under the bridge.

She flipped desperately through her spell
book as D4rkHunter and Rox_Ur_Sox fought

the air giant. The bridge shook as the air giant knocked loose another chunk. It was only a matter of time before it destroyed the whole bridge.

Then Em3ra1d spotted a spell.

She waited for the key to swing back out into view, glittering in the sun. Then she aimed her hand and shouted, *"Levitate!"*

The key began to float upward, tied to the rope like a balloon. The key floated in front of her, and she grabbed it, untied it from the rope, and put it safely in her robe pocket.

But the Air Level wasn't over. They had to find the key *and* defeat the monster.

The air giant was taking damage from the other players' attacks, but it wasn't enough. Everyone was running low on Health and Power. They had to end this, and fast.

She stood up, too focused on the air giant to think about the height of the bridge. *The spell has to work this time.* She aimed both her hands at the air giant and yelled as loud as she could above the howling winds.

"Fireball!"

Green flames shot from her hands and wound around the air giant like a fiery rope. Fueled by the wind that held the air giant together, the flames roared higher and higher. In moments, an enormous tornado of swirling green flames had swallowed the air giant.

Then the air giant exploded. The floating boulders and rocks of the giant's body shot out in a burst of green fire, narrowly missing the players' heads. The players clung tightly to the bridge as the force of the explosion and the wall of rock fragments threatened to knock them all off.

Then the green flames disappeared. The air fell still—all trace of the air giant gone.

They had beaten the air giant. Em3ra1d had the key. Why hadn't the Air Level ended?

A deep rumbling caused the pebbles on the bridge to dance.

They all looked with horror to the end of the bridge where they had started. Piece after piece collapsed into the chasm below. The air giant had weakened the bridge and the explosion had finished it off. Now the whole structure was collapsing.

"Run!" E1_Kapitan shouted as another piece of bridge crumbled and fell.

They all turned and ran as fast as they could for the other end of the bridge.

E1_Kapitan reached the snowy ledge on the far side, then D4rkHunter. Em3rald was close behind them. She had never been so thankful to be back on solid ground.

"Guys!" A panicked shout came from behind them.

Em3rald turned to see Rox_Ur_Sox still running for the end of the bridge. Weighed down by her heavy armor and weapon, she was barely keeping ahead of the collapsing bridge. The rock was crumbling away beneath her feet.

She's not going to make it. Em3rald tried to think of a spell to save her, but she was too low on Power after using *Fireball.* The bridge collapsed beneath Rox_Ur_Sox and she was falling. E1_Kapitan lunged for the edge of the chasm, sticking his staff out to extend his reach. Rox_Ur_Sox's fingers missed it by inches, and she fell into the chasm, her scream echoing.

Unable to do anything else, the rest of the party flopped down on the snowy ground to rest, still breathing heavily. They waited for Rox_Ur_Sox to respawn and for their Health and Power crystals to recharge.

"Tell me something, Em," D4rkHunter said as Rox_Ur_Sox materialized again. "How have you made it this far in life without gaming?"

"Were video games banned in your home?" E1_Kapitan suggested. "I know my *abuela* and I had a hard time convincing my mom that video games wouldn't melt my brain."

"How about you, Roxy?" D4rkHunter asked Rox_Ur_Sox.

"*Pfft!*" she exclaimed. "The only thing keeping me from gaming twenty-four seven is arguing with my sister over whose turn it is." She shrugged. "Aside from, y'know, real-world stuff like school and sleeping."

D4rkHunter looked back at Em3ra1d expectantly.

"I guess I don't know why," Em3rald said. "None of my friends play video games, and I'm always super busy with swim practice or homework."

D4rkHunter grinned and waggled his eyebrows. "But you love gaming *now*, right?"

Em3rald rolled her eyes. "I'll have to get back to you on that," she laughed. "For now, let's just focus on important things like defeating the dragon."

"Agreed," said E1_Kapitan. "Okay guys, this is the Boss Battle. We've totally got this. Just remember to be careful, though. We've all had two deaths, and the third one is permanent. Nobody needs to be a hero; don't do anything stupid or impulsive. We can just hang back and chip away at the dragon. Between the four of us, we should be able to do a lot of damage. And then we'll rescue the princess!"

Rox_Ur_Sox nodded and stood up. "Guess we should head for that cave, then."

"First, I need to use this," said Em3rald, holding up her key. They found her chest

buried in the snow that drifted on the
mountain ledge and unlocked it with her key.
The key vanished with a gust of wind that blew
flurries of snow around them.

But there wasn't a new spell book inside.
Just a scroll.

A single word appeared above the chest:

WISH

Em3ra1d eagerly unrolled the scroll to
learn more about the spell.

The paper was completely blank.

LEVEL 5

BOSS BATTLE

CHAPTER 13

They crept cautiously into the cave, weapons at the ready in case the dragon was lying in wait for them. It was bitterly cold, and their breath hung in the air in puffs of frost. Every surface in the cave glittered. Pillars of ice supported an arched ceiling.

"It looks more like a medieval throne room than a cave," Em3ra1d remarked, keeping her voice low.

"Does anyone see the princess?" Rox_Ur_Sox whispered.

"Look!" D4rkHunter said.

Instead of a throne, a tall block of ice dominated the center of the room. As they got closer, Em3ra1d_with_3nvy gasped. Through the ice, she could see the princess's shiny hair framing her face in perfect ringlets. She was frozen inside the block.

"How do we get her out of there?" asked Em3ra1d.

"Don't even think about using your *Fireball* spell!" Rox_Ur_Sox smirked. "We're supposed to rescue the princess, not barbecue her."

"Oh, shut up," Em3ra1d said, grimacing at her. "What's your plan then?"

In answer, Rox_Ur_Sox took her Volcanic War Hammer and touched it gently to the top of the ice block. The hammer glowed red and the ice began to melt from the top of the block down. It kept melting, even when Rox_Ur_Sox removed her war hammer.

Within moments, the ice had melted enough to uncover the princess's face.

Her eyelids fluttered open, revealing dark, sparkling eyes. "Oh, thank goodness you've come!" she said in a breathy, high-pitched voice.

"Yeah, we're pretty thankful we made it this far too." D4rkHunter wasn't looking at the princess but instead kept scanning the cave uneasily for the dragon.

The ice had melted to the princess's waist now. She was wearing a flowing white dress covered in ruffles and shimmery gauze.

"Not many people make it this far," the princess cooed. "You must indeed be brave and noble adventurers!"

The princess seemed unconcerned about the dragon, but Em3ra1d's skin prickled with goose bumps from more than just the cold. *Am I missing something?* She looked from the mouth of the cave back to the princess. The ice was pooling around the princess's ankles now. The princess smiled sweetly, her eyes light and twinkling. *Didn't her eyes used to be darker?*

"Mmm," the princess sighed, stretching and shaking the last bits of ice off her dress. "That's better."

Nothing happened. There was no sign of a dragon, but the game didn't seem to be over.

"Is that it?" Rox_Ur_Sox asked the princess. "Did the game glitch? I thought we were supposed to rescue you from a dragon."

The princess giggled with a sound of tinkling icicles. "No, silly, the quest was to release the princess *and* defeat the dragon. I never said I was the one who needed rescuing."

There was something wrong with the princess's eyes. They continued to grow paler and paler. White spread across her eyes and pupils like frost covering a windowpane, until her eyes had lost all their color.

"Oh no," Rox_Ur_Sox groaned, backing away. "This can't be good."

They all ran back to the entrance of the ice cave, but bars of ice blocked the way. Rox_Ur_Sox hit them with her Volcanic War Hammer, but even though it had melted the block of ice moments before, it didn't seem to have any effect on the bars. E1_Kapitan tried and failed to pull the bars apart with vines from his staff.

"Going so soon?" the princess growled.

They turned just in time to see the princess grow and morph into a giant ice dragon.

"The princess *is* the dragon?!" E1_Kapitan's eyes widened. "Not cool, man!

Not cool." He used his Shadow Staff to turn invisible.

"Thank you for releasing me," the dragon hissed.

"Don't mention it!" D4rkHunter snapped and shot an arrow at the dragon's chest. The electric arrow left a small scorch mark, but the dragon hardly seemed to notice.

Em3ra1d didn't waste any time. *"Fireball!"*

A ball of green flame flared from her hand and shot toward the dragon. The dragon made a sound somewhere between a roar and a scream, staggering backward as the green flames scorched it and scarred its smooth hide with red burns and gray ash.

But the dragon was still standing.

"It's the Boss Battle," D4rkHunter shouted. "It's not going to be as easy to defeat as the other creatures."

"Those guys were easy?" Em3ra1d said with a nervous laugh.

D4rkHunter dashed forward, another arrow ready to fire from his Spark Bow. Rox_Ur_Sox slammed her Volcanic War

Hammer down onto the dragon's tail. E1_Kapitan was still invisible, but thorny vines appeared and began to wrap around the dragon's legs.

Em3rald kept her distance. She could cast her spells from anywhere, and she didn't have armor to protect her. She was of more use to the other players back here.

She waited for her blue Power crystal to recharge enough to use *Fireball* again. She tapped the blue Power crystal impatiently with her finger, as though that would somehow get it to recharge faster.

The dragon wasn't defeated yet, but it was looking rough from all of their combined attacks. If she could just hit it with *Fireball* again, she felt confident that would finish it off.

Then the dragon roared with a sound like an avalanche. It opened its mouth wide, and a blast of ice and hail came rushing out. The icy breath spread out it in a cloud, enveloping Rox_Ur_Sox and D4rkHunter. It even covered E1_Kapitan and turned him visible again. The icy breath stopped just short of Em3rald.

The other players weren't moving. Em3ra1d's stomach lurched as she realized the dragon's breath had frozen them into statues of glittering ice.

With a swish of its tail, the dragon knocked the three ice statues over. They fell to the ground and broke into jagged chunks of ice before disappearing into pixels. Em3ra1d bit back a scream.

```
ROX_UR_SOX: DEATH 3 OF 3
        GAME OVER


D4RKHUNTER: DEATH 3 OF 3
        GAME OVER


EL_KAPITAN: DEATH 3 OF 3
        GAME OVER
```

CHAPTER 14

Everyone else was gone, and they wouldn't be respawning this time. Em3ra1d was all alone in the game.

She ducked behind an ice pillar, heart pounding, hoping the dragon hadn't seen her. She just needed to hide from the dragon until she could think of a plan.

The dragon laughed. "I know there's one of you left. Now . . . which pillar are you hiding behind?"

Em3ra1d paged through her spell book, her fingers numb and clumsy with cold. She probably only had one chance to finish off the dragon before it got her.

"I'll find you," the dragon said. It sounded bored, as if the battle was already over. "There's no point in hiding from me."

She could hear the dragon's tail swishing over the ice as it stalked its prey. Its steps sounded slow and deliberate. Her stomach sloshed with fear.

Panicked thoughts raced through her mind. What if she used *Fireball* again and it wasn't enough to kill the dragon? She wouldn't have a chance for her blue Power crystal to recharge before the dragon got her with its ice breath. Game over.

"Come out, come out, wherever you are!" the dragon hummed, a sound like the slushy patter of sleet against a window.

She felt the blank spell scroll in her pocket. The message had said "wish." *But what does that mean? How am I supposed to use it?* She could hear the dragon getting closer.

The dragon's head appeared around the pillar, one large glittering white eye staring at her. "Found you," the dragon said with a low cackle.

"*Wish*!" screamed Em3ra1d, desperate to at least try *something*. "I wish my friends were back in the game!"

D4rkHunter, Rox_Ur_Sox, and E1_Kapitan respawned immediately in various places around the cave.

Instead of draining Em3ra1d's Power, casting *Wish* had recharged her Power crystal. It was now glowing bright blue.

"*Fireball*!" she yelled as loud as she could before the dragon had time to react.

The ball of green flame whooshed into the dragon's face. The dragon reared back on its hind legs, and three of D4rkHunter's arrows lodged in its belly, sparking with purple lightning. Rox_Ur_Sox swung her war hammer at the dragon's tree-trunk-sized hind legs. The war hammer glowed bright red and made a sizzling sound as it made contact with the ice dragon's scales. E1_Kapitan shot thorn darts from his staff. The darts hit the dragon's wings, shredding them into ribbons.

With a loud cracking sound like cold glass

breaking in hot water, the dragon disappeared in a shower of snowflake-shaped pixels.

VICTORY

Rox_Ur_Sox whooped with joy and hugged Em3ra1d tight. "Good work, n00b!" she said, smiling broadly. "How did we come back? I thought it was three strikes, you're out."

"The scroll I got for defeating the Air Level was a spell called *Wish*. So I wished you all back in the game."

"For real?" El_Kapitan punched Em3ra1d gently in the arm. "Let me get this straight, you had the ability to wish for *anything*, and you didn't just wish for the dragon to be defeated?"

Em3ra1d laughed, embarrassed that she hadn't thought of that. "Uh, yeah, I thought of that—*obviously*—but I didn't want you guys to be trapped in the game forever. And besides, where's the reward in just *wishing* for victory?"

They walked to the back of the cave to try to find the exit. Rox_Ur_Sox leaned in close to Em3ra1d and whispered, "You totally just panicked and wished for the first thing that came into your head, didn't you?"

"Totally," Em3ra1d admitted.

"That's my n00b," Rox_Ur_Sox said, smiling.

"Actually," Em3ra1d said, raising the volume of her voice so the guys could hear her too, "my real name is—"

"No!" the other three shouted at once.

"No real names in the game," E1_Kapitan explained.

D4rkHunter nodded. "Yeah, you can tell us later, in the real world."

"Oh. Okay." Em3ra1d chewed the side of her lip to hide the smile growing. *Guess this means we're staying in touch after the game ends.*

At the back of the cave, they found the Game Runner, still wearing his white suit and sunglasses.

"Good work!" he said as they approached. "You beat the game! I have to say, the programmers are pretty proud of the twist ending where the princess *is* the dragon. Be honest: did you see it coming? I'm surprised you noticed the change in her eyes—"

"Can we go now?" D4rkHunter interrupted. "We beat the game."

The Game Runner gestured to the back of the cave with his hand, and a door that hadn't been there a moment ago swung open. "Just exit the game through there when you're ready. Unfortunately, the L33T C0RP gift shop isn't open in beta, but there will be an exciting survey to fill out about your experience, so let us know how we're doing!"

The players were all heading for the door, when something in the snow caught Em3ra1d's eye. She bent down to pick it up. A crystal key gleamed in her hand. Em3ra1d looked at the Game Runner. He didn't say anything, but the corner of his mouth twitched into a smile.

"Guys, wait!" Em3ra1d called after her friends. "Look what I found!"

They gathered around her.

"It's a fifth key," Rox_Ur_Sox gasped.

"What do you think it unlocks?" asked D4rkHunter.

A message popped into the air:

DO YOU WISH TO CONTINUE?
YES/NO

"We could keep playing?" E1_Kapitan asked, raising his eyebrows.

The Game Runner nodded. "You've fulfilled your original contract by winning the game. From here on out, you're welcome to keep playing as volunteer beta testers. Of course you'll need to sign a waiver—"

D4rkHunter turned to the Game Runner. "But we could still leave whenever we want, right?"

"Certainly. Even if you lose a game, you can now exit at any time."

"Well, how about it, Em?" Rox_Ur_Sox asked. "Are you sick of us yet?"

"You guys would *want* me to keep playing?" Em3rald asked.

"Of course," D4rkHunter said.

"We'd be screwed without a good Mage," Rox_Ur_Sox added with a smirk.

"But don't feel like we're pressuring you," E1_Kapitan told her. "I know you said gaming wasn't really your scene."

Em3ra1d looked at the crystal key in her hand, and then her friends.

A smile slowly spread across her face.

GAME
OVER

WHAT WOULD YOU DO IF YOU WOKE UP IN A VIDEO GAME?

CHECK OUT ALL OF THE TITLES IN THE

LEVEL UP

SERIES